THE NEW TENANT

ACORN BOOKS No 29

THE
NEW TENANT

by
FLORENCE FOSTER

VICTORY PRESS
LONDON AND EASTBOURNE

© VICTORY PRESS 1958

First published in this Series 1967

ISBN 085476 103 9

Printed in Great Britain for
VICTORY PRESS (Evangelical Publishers Ltd.),
Lottbridge Drove, Eastbourne, Sussex,
by Compton Printing Ltd.,
Aylesbury, Bucks.

CHAPTER ONE

SAYING GOOD-BYE

A FEELING of excitement filled Sheila as she took a last look round the little room, now so unfamiliar, with its bare walls and floor.

Downstairs she could hear the tread of heavy feet and the sound of men's voices as they moved the furniture from the house to the waiting van, and, crossing the room, she pushed open the casement window and looked down on the busy scene below. Furniture, shrouded in sacking, half filled the large van, and several more articles were lying around waiting to be packed away and conveyed to their new home.

Leaning far out of the window, she could just see, through the almost leafless trees, the roof and chimney-pots of Southernwood, so soon to be her home. Sheila had longed for this day to arrive. Drawing back from her precarious position, she settled herself more comfortably on the window-sill and her thoughts went back over the past year.

It was hard to imagine that only a year ago Southernwood had stood silent and empty save for Old Jake, the caretaker and gardener, and that Sheila herself had been lonely and unhappy. But now things were very different; since the return of Mrs. Denholme, Southernwood's owner, with her grandson Peter, everything had changed.

The noisy slamming of the van door brought Sheila back to the present. Pulling the window to and fastening it securely, she jumped down from the sill and crossed to the door.

"Good-bye, little room," she said softly, her hand on the door-knob. "I hope you have someone nice to live in you. I wonder who it will be?"

Running downstairs, she joined her mother in the hall and, gathering up the small packages that remained, they let themselves out of the house and made their way to Southernwood. The van was already there, and the workmen had started to unload when Sheila and Mrs. Carliss arrived on the scene. Carefully avoiding the workmen with their heavy loads, Sheila went to find her father. He was helping Jake to lay the carpets in the large suite of rooms that Mrs. Denholme had set apart for Sheila and her parents. Standing in the doorway of the dining-room, a spacious room with oak-beamed ceiling and latticed windows, Sheila watched Jake and her father as they worked. In the large, open fireplace a log fire was crackling merrily and sending out a welcoming glow in bright contrast to the grey January skies outside.

"Tea is ready, Sheila," called a gentle voice, and Sheila turned quickly to see Mrs. Denholme standing behind her. Anyone less like a grandmother than Nanette would be hard to imagine; she was dainty and charming and, Sheila thought, the prettiest grandmother anyone could ever wish to have.

"Oh, Nanette," exclaimed Sheila happily, tucking her arm into Nanette's, "I'm going to love being here; it's like home already."

Mrs. Denholme gave her a quick little hug. "I want you all to be very happy," she replied, then, calling to Sheila's parents, she led the way to her own drawing-room, where, with her usual thoughtfulness, she had had a meal prepared for her tired and hungry guests.

Waiting for them, curled up in his favourite armchair, was

"Smoky", no longer the helpless little kitten that Sheila and Peter had once saved from drowning, but grown into a beautiful cat very aware of his attractiveness. Smoky had entrenched himself firmly in Nanette's domain. He opened a sleepy eye in answer to Sheila's greeting and caress, then curled himself up tighter, as if daring her to move him from his comfortable position.

Sheila laughed and settled herself on a large hassock by the fire.

"All right, Smoky, you are quite safe as far as I am concerned, but I don't know what Nanette will say when she sees you."

Nanette said little, but gently and firmly picked him up and put him in the cosy basket that was his rightful place. With an air of offended dignity, Smoky promptly climbed out and, crossing to the door, asked imperiously for it to be opened.

Nanette and Sheila were soon joined by Sheila's parents, and after a simple grace they began their tea.

"I wonder who will come to live in our little house now," remarked Sheila, voicing the thought that had been in her mind ever since she had heard they were leaving the cottage to live in Southernwood.

"No-one very exciting, I'm afraid, Sheila," answered Mr. Carliss. "Just a retired business man who wants to live very quietly."

"Oh!" Sheila's face showed her disappointment. "How dull! I'd hoped there might be someone of my own age."

"Never mind, dear," consoled her mother, "the Easter holidays are not so very far away, and then you will have Peter home again."

Sheila brightened at the thought. Peter was fun, and there was never a dull moment when he was home, but all the same it would be nice to have someone to share the weeks between the holidays.

When tea was over she left her parents and Nanette talking round the fire and ran down the long stone corridor that led to Jake's apartments.

"Come in, Missy," called out a cheery voice in answer to her knock.

"How did you know it was me?" asked Sheila, as she closed the door behind her.

The old man chuckled.

"No-one else trips along quite like you do," he assured her. "Also 'tis your usual time, or thereabouts, for calling. But come and sit down, and a very special welcome, as it's your first day in Southernwood."

He drew forward a chair. "I've already got one visitor," he announced, nodding towards the chair nearest the fireside.

Sheila looked, and there, a triumphant gleam in his eyes, sat Smoky, purring softly and contentedly.

A few days later, returning from school, Sheila noticed with interest and not a little excitement that curtains were hanging at the windows of her old home and a thin spiral of smoke curled lazily from the chimney of the living-room. The new tenant had arrived.

The weeks passed uneventfully. Sheila's parents and Nanette, with the help of Hannah and Betty, were busily preparing the hitherto unused rooms of Southernwood in readiness for the guests who would be arriving in the summer.

Sheila looked forward to the springtime, when the gentle rains and warm sunshine would transform the bleak landscape into leafy woods and flowering hedgerows. The moors that stretched for miles around the village would lose their gaunt and lonely appearance and glow with the gold and purple of gorse and heather. Another month and Peter would be home for the Easter holidays and they would be able to explore the countryside together and revisit favourite haunts.

An exclamation from her father, who was reading the morning newspaper, interrupted Sheila's day-dreams.

"What is it, dear?" asked Mrs. Carliss from the other side of the breakfast table.

"A convict has escaped from Downly Prison," replied her husband. "Rather a dangerous fellow, it seems. He is serving a sentence for robbery with violence."

Sheila's mother looked alarmed. "Oh, dear, I hope he doesn't come this way," she said apprehensively.

"Don't worry, my dear," reassured Mr. Carliss, "the police believe he is making for London. In any case, Downly is nearly thirty miles from here, and I don't suppose he will get far before the police catch him."

Somewhat relieved Mrs. Carliss resumed her breakfast and Mr. Carliss continued to read his paper. Sheila, who had finished her meal, slipped from her chair and looked over her father's shoulder to read the startling piece of news. The grim, set face of a young man stared back at her.

Cycling along the road that led to Dunston and Brownstones School, Sheila's thoughts were of the unfortunate man whose misdeeds had put him in prison and who was now in hiding from the police. Last summer, when motoring across the moors with Nanette and Peter, she had seen the prison, a grey, gaunt, fortress-like building, and she shuddered at the depressing memory.

When she reached school the playground was a-buzz with chatter as groups of excited girls discussed the latest news.

"Do you think he will come this way?" asked Jean Murray hopefully.

"No," answered Betty Talbot; "he's safe in London by now. My father thinks he had someone to help him get away."

"The police stopped our bus this morning to see if we had the escaped convict on board," put in another.

"Oo—oh, weren't you scared?"—and so the excited chatter went on until the school bell summoned them inside.

Only Margaret Hammet remained quiet and disinterested. Usually she was in the foreground of every discussion, and her remarks were often far from kind, as Sheila had good cause to remember. But for once she seemed anxious to remain unnoticed.

The next day a strange rumour started. Who began it no-one knew, but it gradually gained strength until the whole school was whispering and talking about it.

"Have you heard?" whispered Betty Talbot to Sheila in class; "the escaped convict is Margaret's uncle."

Sheila looked startled.

"I don't believe it. It's just a silly rumour."

"All right, let's ask her at break and see if she denies it," replied the other, and later, when they were released from their studies for a brief spell, a crowd of girls surrounded the hapless Margaret and questioned her outright.

White-faced and miserable, Margaret tried to evade their questions, but mercilessly they persisted until, in tears, she admitted that it was true. The missing convict was her mother's youngest brother.

A wave of indignation swept the crowd of girls standing round.

"She ought not to be allowed to stay at Brownstones," said one; "it's letting the school down."

"Just wait until my parents know about this," added another; "they'll be writing to Miss Fellows, for sure."

"What a come-down for Margaret, after all her airs and graces," remarked a third, a girl who was one of Margaret's especial set; and one by one Margaret's former friends, ignoring her appealing look for support, drifted away.

"Oh, what a shame!" cried Sheila indignantly, her grey eyes flashing. Quickly she went to Margaret's side and turned to face the unfriendly crowd. "Margaret hasn't done anything wrong; it's not her fault that her uncle has been sent to prison."

But the other girls were not so sure and, still talking amongst themselves, they slowly walked away, leaving Sheila and Margaret together.

"Never mind, Margaret," said Sheila stoutly; "I think it's a jolly shame, and if they want to be beastly to you, they can be beastly to me, too."

Margaret looked at her gratefully. "It's good of you to stand up for me, Sheila, especially after the horrid way I once treated you," she answered shakily.

Sheila laughed and took Margaret's arm—a friendly gesture.

"A lot has happened since then. One day I'll tell you about it."

Margaret looked at her curiously. Sheila had certainly changed during the past year, and Margaret would have given a great deal to know the reason.

In spite of one or two indignant letters from outraged parents, Miss Fellows did not ask for Margaret to be removed from Brownstones, and after a few days the gossip and scandal died down, but the friendship between Sheila and Margaret remained.

CHAPTER TWO

SHEILA'S ADVENTURE

SEATED in front of the blazing log fire, Smoky curled up between them, Sheila and Margaret chatted happily. Mrs. Carliss had invited Margaret to tea, and now, after one of the most enjoyable evenings she could remember, Margaret was waiting for Sheila's father to take her home. She had been introduced to Nanette, taken to visit Jake in his cosy rooms and then shown some of the treasures of Southernwood. The long gallery, with its portraits and carvings, its rare tapestries and priceless china and curios, was like a museum and had fascinated her. Nanette had been delighted with the interest she had shown.

"You must come again, my dear, and be my little guest," she said kindly.

"Oh, lovely, Nanette!" exclaimed Sheila, taking her own invitation for granted. "Can it be during the holidays, when Peter is home?"

And Nanette had agreed.

Margaret reached out her hand and stroked Smoky's head, causing him to purr louder than ever.

"You know, Sheila," she said slowly, "if—if my uncle hadn't gone to prison and the other girls at school hadn't been so horrid to me, you and I would never have become friends. Isn't it strange that sometimes the most unpleasant things can lead to the nicest?"

"Blessings in disguise," remarked a cheery voice behind

them, and Margaret turned and looked up into the smiling face of Mr. Carliss, who had entered the room in time to over-hear her remark. "That's the way God often works in our lives, Margaret."

Not for the first time during her brief visit, Margaret felt a keen sense of curiosity and surprise. This family of Sheila's spoke of God as if He were a personal Friend, interested in everything they did.

Sheila ran off to fetch their out-door clothes while Margaret took her leave of Mrs. Carliss, then together they made their way out to the waiting car.

"Tumble in," Sheila's father called out gaily, "and I'll have you home in no time."

The next day Sheila wheeled her bicycle out of the school shed and was about to mount when an odd bumpiness made her look down. The back tyre was ominously flat.

"Oh, dear," she sighed; "I hope it's not a puncture."

But after several minutes of pumping that made not the slightest impression, she examined the tyre and found a sharp piece of flint firmly embedded in the outer cover.

"This means I'll be late home for tea," she thought rue-fully; "but it can't be helped. I'll just have to take it along to Mr. Soames and ask him to mend it."

Wishing that she had learned to mend punctures herself, instead of leaving them to Jake or her father, Sheila pushed her bicycle out of the school gates and down the road to the small garage a short distance away. But when she reached it the doors of the garage were firmly closed. Sheila went round to the small shop attached to the garage, but that, too, was closed, and a notice on the door announced the fact that it was early closing day.

Sheila looked at her watch and groaned. The hands pointed to four-thirty, and the last bus to go anywhere near Southernwood left at four twenty-five. There was nothing else to do but walk the four miles to her home. Propping her bicycle against the wall, out of sight of the road and well sheltered from the weather, she set off.

The first mile went pleasantly enough, but by the end of the second Sheila was beginning to feel a bit weary and decidedly hungry. She plodded on until presently she came to where a footpath branched off from the main road. It was a short cut to Southernwood, and if she took it instead of keeping to the main road, it would shorten the rest of her journey by half. Sheila pondered for a few moments. It was not a way she usually took, for it was only a rough and stony track across the edge of the moor and considered dangerous. There were open, derelict quarries into which people, unused to the district and wandering from the track, had sometimes fallen. But Sheila knew the part well, and deciding she would have plenty of time to get across before darkness fell, turned left into the track.

She had gone barely half way when she began to doubt the wisdom of her choice. The loose, mossy stones beneath her feet made progress slow and difficult, while dark clouds, blowing in from the sea, brought with them a chilling sea mist. But having come so far, there was no point in turning back, so she trudged on steadily.

Then, without warning, in the terrifyingly sudden way that moor and sea mists have, the landscape was blotted out with a thick white blanket.

Sheila stood still, not knowing what to do, then moved warily forward. It was foolish to be stranded on the moors only a quarter of a mile from her home. If she was careful she would soon come to the end of the track and be safe on the main road again.

But the moors in a thick mist can be very treacherous, and not until Sheila felt the ground giving way beneath her feet in the most sickening manner did she realise that she had wandered off the footpath. Frantically she threw her arms out in an effort to save herself, but she pitched and rolled down a steep incline until a stout hawthorn bush stopped her progress. Bruised and shaken, she sat up very gingerly and peered around to try to see the extent of her danger. She had undoubtedly fallen over the edge of a disused quarry, but just how much further it was to the bottom she had no idea. Some of the quarries were known to be at least one hundred feet deep, and Sheila held on tightly to the bush that had proved such a friend. To attempt to climb back might prove disastrous, and yet the thought of hours, perhaps the whole night, in that precarious position filled her with dread. She knew her father and Jake would come to look for her as soon as they realised she was lost, but it might be ages before they found her.

Rather forlornly she began to shout.

"Help! help!" she called, then nearly fell from her insecure perch as a voice nearby answered her.

"Keep shouting," called a man's voice; "it will lead me to you."

Sheila continued to shout, and soon she heard cautious movements, and some loose stones rolled past her on their way to the foot of the quarry. Presently a figure loomed up out of the mist in front of her, a strong hand grasped her arm and a voice said reassuringly, "Hold on to me tightly. I'll soon have you to the top."

Thankfully Sheila did as she was told, and step by step they cautiously made their way upwards. Breathless, they reached firm ground at the top of the quarry and Sheila, gasping out her thanks, looked up into the face of her rescuer.

As she did so her words froze in horror.

Looking down at her was the face she had seen on the front page of the morning newspaper several days before. Her rescuer was none other than the escaped convict!

"Why are you staring at me like that?" demanded the man sharply.

"You—you are——" stammered Sheila, struggling to fight down her panic.

"Well?"

"You are Andrew Tennant," she answered, more calmly, "the escaped——"

The man caught her arm in a grip that hurt.

"Now listen to me," he commanded in a harsh voice. "If you are sensible you'll forget you've ever seen me. I've just saved you from a very nasty predicament and you can show your gratitude by keeping quiet about it. Do you understand?"

Sheila nodded and continued to stare at her rescuer. Suddenly she realised she was not afraid of this man who was supposed to be dangerous. There was something about him that was strangely out of keeping with Sheila's idea of a convict. He looked rough and unshaven and his clothes were muddy and torn, but there had been something about his voice when first she heard it that was kind and reassuring and the firm grip of his hand when he pulled her to safety had filled her with confidence.

"I don't think you did it," she burst out.

The man looked at her in amazement.

"Don't think I did what?" he questioned, the harshness in his voice replaced by surprise.

"I don't think you attacked that man and stole all that money. You're much too nice."

Andrew Tennant gave her a long, strange look.

"You are a very discerning young lady," he remarked at length. "As a matter of fact I didn't do it, but I don't expect anyone to believe me." Then, changing the subject abruptly, he went on: — "We can't stand here. There is a large rock a few yards away; I think I can find my way to it. We will sit there and shelter until the mist clears or someone comes to find you."

"What will you do then?" asked Sheila curiously.

"Disappear," replied the man tersely, "and trust you not to give me away."

Together they made their way to the rock and settled themselves as comfortably as they could beneath its shelter. The man sat silent, and Sheila, afraid of annoying him by appearing too curious, held back the questions she longed to ask.

"Do you know a place called 'Southernwood Cottage'?" asked her companion suddenly.

"Why, yes," answered Sheila in surprise "That's where I used to live. We live next door in Southernwood itself now," she added.

"You've got a new neighbour?"

"Why, yes," said Sheila again, wondering how this man knew so much. "Mr. Arnold."

"He's the man I'm supposed to have robbed—with violence," stated Andrew Tennant bitterly, then, seeing her expression of utter bewilderment, he continued: —"We worked for the same firm. He was the senior cashier. One day a large sum of money was missing, and he accused me of attacking him and taking it; but I have my suspicions of what happened to that money." He fell silent, and Sheila looked up into his hard, set face. "He's a clever, ruthless man. I broke out of prison with the foolish notion that I could make him own up, but I've not done myself any good, only added to the length of my sentence."

"How did you know Mr. Arnold was living in Southernwood Cottage?" asked Sheila.

"Quite by accident; a mutual friend mentioned it in a letter a week or two ago. It was that that gave me the idea of breaking out of prison."

He fell silent again, and Sheila said sympathetically, "I wish I could do something to help you prove your innocence."

The man laughed shortly.

"There's not much you can do, I'm afraid, youngster."

"I could pray about it," replied Sheila thoughtfully.

"You could *what?*" queried the man, with tolerant amusement.

"I could pray," repeated Sheila firmly. "God does answer if you love Him and believe that He will."

"Go on," exclaimed her companion, leaning back against the rock and looking at her, but his tone was no longer amused. "What makes you so sure?"

"I just know it's true," said Sheila; "I've proved it."

"I used to think like that once," remarked the man musingly. "I used to go to Sunday School and sing in the choir; in fact, when I was little older than you I had thoughts of training for the ministry. But look at me now"—the bitterness came back into his voice—"I look a long way from such things to-day, don't I? If there is a God, why did He let this happen to me?"

It was too big a question for anyone as young as Sheila to answer and she said slowly, "I don't know—but God does work in ways which seem very strange to us. We find out later that He has been working for our good all the time."

"You are very sure, aren't you?" observed the man kindly. Then he sighed heavily. "I wish I had your faith."

"I wish you had, too," responded Sheila earnestly. "You could have, you know." She paused, then asked shyly, "If God answers my prayers for you will you believe in Him again?"

Andrew Tennant looked down into her bright, eager face.

"All right, youngster," he replied at length, "I promise. It doesn't seem quite right to bargain with God, but if He does answer your prayers, I promise to believe in Him again." He broke off, then said in an undertone that Sheila could scarcely hear, "It might be worth trying, anyway."

They sat in silence for awhile, the thick mist swirling round them. It was getting late, and Sheila wondered if her parents were very anxious. Then, almost as suddenly as it had come, the mist began to clear. Sheila and her companion watched hopefully as nearer objects took on a vague, ghostly shape, then gradually grew solid and real.

"I think, with care, we could reach the main road," proposed the man, standing up and helping Sheila to her feet. "I'll see you to the end of the track, then you will be safe."

Walking carefully, for by now the falling darkness was taking the place of mist, the two finally reached the edge of the moors and the safety of the main road. Here Sheila turned to thank her companion and to say good-bye, but he had disappeared silently and completely.

Knowing how anxious her parents would now be, Sheila broke into a run and reached home just as her father was getting out the car to go and look for her.

"I had a puncture and then got held up by the fog," explained Sheila breathlessly, feeling very guilty at not confiding the whole story to her parents. But a promise was a promise.

The following day, however, the need for secrecy was over. The local paper announced the news that Andrew Tennant had given himself up to the police and had been taken back to Downly Prison. But Sheila still kept her secret to herself. Peter must be the first to hear of her thrilling experience and the promise she had made.

CHAPTER THREE

PETER TAKES COMMAND

SHEILA ran through the little thicket that divided Southernwood from the cottage and, climbing the mossy bank, stood on tip-toe and peered through the thick laurel hedge. The garden of the cottage at first appeared empty, but after a few moments Sheila heard a rustling in the bushes a few yards away and saw a large alsatian dog nosing amongst the undergrowth. As if sensing her presence, it crossed the garden and came growling to the spot where she stood hidden.

"What is it, Bruce?" called an irritable voice, and Mr. Arnold, the new tenant, came into view. He was a man of slight build with a pale face and tight, thin lips. His eyes, pale blue and deep set, were hard and cold as pebbles. Sheila gave a little shiver and quietly withdrew. She had no wish to meet Mr. Arnold or his unfriendly dog just then.

The next day Peter and his parents were due to arrive, and Southernwood was in a state of happy anticipation. Promptly at four, with a crunch of tyres on the gravel drive, their car drew up outside the front entrance and Nanette insisted that everyone should have tea together in her large drawing-room, so that they could talk of all that had happened since last they met.

Tea over, and leaving the adults still talking, Sheila and Peter slipped away.

"Now, Elf," began Peter, using the nick-name he had given her on their first encounter, "tell me about all these mysterious happenings you've been hinting at in your letters."

So Sheila told him about the new tenant and the escaped convict and of her own adventure on the moor.

Peter looked at her with admiration and envy.

"You have had an exciting time," he exclaimed. "Who would think so much could happen in sleepy old Southernwood!"

"It's not sleepy," retorted Sheila, rushing to the defence of her beloved Southernwood.

"All right," laughed Peter, "I agree; it's not sleepy. In fact," he added dramatically, "it seems to be a place of mystery, intrigue and suspicion!"

Sheila looked at him sharply.

"Now you are laughing at me."

"Honestly, Elf, I'm not," declared Peter. "I'm thrilled with the whole thing. I wish we could do something to help your convict."

"I promised to pray for him."

The fun and teasing died out of Peter's eyes.

"It worked in a wonderful way last year, when we prayed for your parents, didn't it, Elf?" he said quietly, and Sheila nodded.

The next day was Good Friday, and they spent it very quietly. After attending morning service in the little church in the village, Sheila and Peter strolled to the large oak-tree, a favourite spot of theirs and the scene of their first meeting. The air was soft and warm and filled with the scents and sounds of spring. Around them in the trees and bushes the birds kept up a continuous chorus of song, and occasionally a little woodland creature would peep out from the undergrowth and watch them with bright, curious eyes. The fields, sloping down to the sea, were sprinkled with buttercups and snow-white daisies, and where the early bluebells were opening the banks and hedgerows shimmered with blue.

Peter took a deep breath.

"It's good to be back, Sheila. There is nowhere quite so beautiful as Southernwood."

They sat without speaking, watching the cloud-shadows as they drifted across the fields and sea, and a vole, deceived by the silence, ran out of the grass, then stopped abruptly and eyed them with beady suspicion. Cautiously Peter felt in his pocket for a crumb of biscuit, but at the slight movement the little creature darted back into the long grass.

"I'm getting hungry," announced Peter. "It must be nearly lunch-time. Race you to the house." And springing to his feet he sped away, with Sheila in close pursuit.

The following day as they climbed the steps that led from the beach, Peter asked, "When are we going to start looking for evidence to clear your convict?"

Sheila ruefully admitted that she did not know.

"We shall have to plan a campaign," declared Peter. "First we must get on friendly terms with Mr. Arnold, then get him talking and hope he gives himself away. In the meantime we must keep a sharp look-out for any suitable hiding-places or anything that looks suspicious."

Having seen Mr. Arnold, Sheila thought that any chances of getting on friendly terms with him were very remote, but she was willing to try, and accordingly that afternoon they decided to call on him. Reaching the front gate, they stopped to tidy themselves a little, then walked boldly up the path to the door.

At the sound of their footsteps the alsatian came rushing round the corner of the house, barking furiously.

"Nice old boy," said Peter soothingly, stooping to pat him, but the dog snapped and snarled and Peter hastily withdrew his hand.

They continued up the path, the dog still growling at their heels, and as they were about to knock, the door was flung open and they were confronted by Mr. Arnold, looking far from pleased to see them.

"What do you want?" he demanded.

"We've just come to call on you, sir," answered Peter politely. "We are your neighbours and—and we thought we would like to be friendly."

"Well, you can just go away again," responded their neighbour ungraciously. "I've no time to waste on social calls. Bruce, come here, sir!"

Reluctantly the dog obeyed, and with a last defiant growl went into the house.

"I used to live here," ventured Sheila quickly, as the door began to close. "I could tell you quite a lot——"

"I'm not interested in where you used to live," broke in Mr. Arnold, "and I've no time for idle chatter." With which remark he firmly closed the door in their faces.

"Well!" ejaculated Peter, "we don't seem to be very welcome, do we?"

Feeling rather weak, Sheila leaned against the wall of the porch and laughed helplessly.

"What's the next move in your campaign, General?" she managed to ask at length.

"Tea," answered the General promptly. "I need it. We will come back to the attack next week."

The fine, warm weather continued over the week-end. Sunday, of course, was spent attending the Easter Day services, but on the Monday someone suggested a picnic on the moors.

"Why not ask Margaret to come?" suggested Nanette, and Sheila ran off to ring her friend and make arrangements to meet her on the way to the moors.

Dr. Glennie, Peter and Sheila drove off in the first car, leaving a vacant seat for Margaret, while Mr. Carliss and the three ladies followed. On the back of each car was strapped a substantial hamper.

Just outside the village, Margaret, looking happy and excited, was waiting for them. Dr. Glennie drew up, and Margaret joined Sheila in the back of the car, then they sped on their way again. Turning off the main road to miss the town, they drove down leafy, winding lanes, over narrow bridges and streams, past quaint, thatched cottages and farms and eventually reached open country with the moors stretching out before them. The road lay straight ahead and ran like a white ribbon into the distance. Moorland ponies, grazing by the roadside, looked at them curiously as they passed, but when, at Peter's request, Dr. Glennie stopped the car and the three children tried to coax the ponies nearer, the wild creatures galloped off to the safety of the moors.

"When are we stopping for a picnic, Uncle John?" asked Sheila presently.

"I don't know, Sheila," replied Dr. Glennie. "We just thought we would drive along until we found somewhere pleasant. Let's wait for the others to catch up with us and hear what they say."

The other car soon came into sight and drew up beside them.

"I believe there is a pretty little spot not far from here," said Sheila's father. "I remember coming this way some time ago and, if my memory doesn't fail me, we should turn left a few hundred yards ahead. I'll go first and lead the way."

Turning off the main road once more, they ran down a steep, narrow lane, the branches of the trees meeting overhead and forming a green canopy that almost shut out the daylight. To their right, through the trees, they caught glimpses of a moorland stream that rushed and foamed over the grey boulders and seemed to be trying to race them on their journey to the valley below.

After a few minutes they emerged again into the sunshine and drew up, entranced. The stream lay before them, playful and sparkling in the sunlight; an old bridge, mellowed by centuries, spanned it, while boulders made stepping-stones to the wooded bank on the other side. A wide stretch of smooth grass sloped down to where the water gently lapped the silver-grey sand, and all agreed that it was the perfect spot for a picnic.

The fresh moorland air had given everyone a keen appetite by this time, and while Peter helped his father and Mr. Carliss to light the stove to boil the kettle, Sheila and Margaret assisted by spreading the snowy-white table-cloth on the ground and placing the contents of the hampers on it. Such a spread confronted them when they sat down, and after Dr. Glennie had given thanks they set to with a will until the plates of sandwiches and cakes and biscuits were nearly empty. Then, the meal over and everything cleared away, Sheila, Margaret and Peter decided to follow the course of the stream.

Round boulders and under overhanging branches of weeping-willow trees it foamed and frolicked, calling them on and on. Occasionally they came to a pool between the rocks where the water was clear and still and the silver sand on the stream's bed sparkled in the sun, and once they caught sight of a large brown trout lurking in the shadows, but when Peter tried to catch it, it shot away out of his grasp. When the stream ran shallow over a bed of boulders they clambered across to the other side and, breathless with exertion, dropped down on the mossy bank. For a while they sat and chatted, then, deciding that the others would be getting anxious if they stayed away too long, they climbed back over the rocks and retraced their steps. They had not gone very far when they saw Sheila's father with Dr. Glennie coming to meet them.

"We were coming to find you to tell you it will soon be time to leave," said Mr. Carliss. "We are going home by a longer route, which will give us a closer view of the Tors."

Pleased at the prospect of getting a close view of the strange, massive formation of rocks, many of which were scattered over the moors and were the source of strange tales and legends, the three raced back to the waiting cars. After a last look round to see they had not left any litter to spoil the loveliness of the little spot where they had picnicked, they all climbed in and drove away.

The road ran uphill and down between stretches of sweeping moorland. Now and again they passed an isolated cottage or farm and once, in the distance, Sheila caught a glimpse of the grey, fortress prison. With a little ache in her heart she wondered how her convict friend was faring. But the car sped on, the prison was lost to view, and soon the little party was looking with awe and wonder at the great rocks that stood like giant sentinels against the evening sky.

CHAPTER FOUR

ANDREW'S DECISION

SEATED on a narrow bed in a small, cell-like room, lighted only by a window set in the high wall, Andrew Tennant was deep in thought.

After his meeting with Sheila he had spent another night on the moors, getting what shelter he could from the pitiless damp and cold, and when morning came, bringing with it a keen east wind and the realisation of the futility of his action in breaking out of prison, he gave himself up to the police.

On his return to Downly Prison, Andrew had been weak and ill from exposure and lack of food, and the medical officer had sent him straight to the sick-bay. There he had long hours of solitude in which to think, and he dwelt continually on the conversation he had had with Sheila. He could not forget her earnest little face and her confident faith that God would put all things right for him. His mind travelled back to the days when he, too, had professed belief in God. But what a shallow thing his profession had been ! As soon as he had left College and entered the world of business he had drifted away from the Church, away from God. He had been caught up in the excitement and keen competition of money-making and commerce. Good-natured and easy-going, he had soon become the centre of a smart young set, and in their company he had been introduced to the pleasures and temptations of city life.

His thoughts were interrupted by the turning of the key in the lock, and the prison chaplain, grey-haired but tall and upright, with an almost military bearing, was ushered in. Andrew had asked that he might see him, and the prison officer, though surprised, had speedily granted his request. He rose to meet the padre as he entered, and found his hand taken in a hard, strong grip.

The padre looked into the face of the young prisoner before him and was surprised and pleased at what he saw. Underlying strength of character and humour were quickly detected by the keen eyes of the chaplain, who in his long years of prison service had met and spoken with men of many different types and personalities.

Drawing up a plain wooden chair and indicating to Andrew to re-seat himself on the side of the bed, he asked the question uppermost in his mind.

"What are you doing here, my boy?"

"You know my record, sir?" inquired Andrew quietly.

"Yes, indeed I do," replied the padre gravely, "but it doesn't fit in with what I see. Tell me all about it."

And Andrew found himself pouring out the whole sorry story.

"I'd got myself into a bit of a mess, sir. With gambling and drinking and generally living beyond my means I'd got myself pretty heavily in debt, and people were pressing me for payment. Then I had a lucky break, if you can call it that. I made quite a bit at the races, and was able to pay off most of the debts. That night, at the office, Arnold was found in a dazed condition and declared that I had attacked and robbed him of the firm's wages. But I swear, sir, I never touched the man or the money."

He looked straight into the face of the older man, and tears were not far from his eyes. The padre laid a kindly hand on his shoulder.

"I believe you, my boy," he said quietly, "I believe you."

He stayed chatting with Andrew for a little longer, then, promising to visit him again, he left him and went straight to the office of the prison Governor. The Governor, younger than the chaplain, but equal in stature and with the stern expression of one who exerts authority, listened as his visitor recounted his interview with Andrew.

"I'm sure that young man is innocent," concluded the padre.

"My dear chap," replied the Governor with a smile, "they all protest their innocence. The evidence against Andrew Tennant is very strong. He says he won the money gambling, but no-one has come forward to corroborate his statement. If only these young fellows would realise that the first easy steps into wrong-doing can have such dire results."

"Is there nothing you can do to help him?" queried the other man.

"Nothing, I'm afraid," rejoined the Governor. "When he has served his sentence we will do all we can to help him make a fresh start; until then he must take his punishment."

Feeling disappointed, the padre left the office; there seemed to be little hope of help from that direction. But man's need was God's opportunity, he knew, and going to his study, he prayed long and earnestly that God would undertake for Andrew.

He saw his prayers partially answered in the days that followed. He and Andrew had many talks together about spiritual things, and Andrew began to look forward eagerly to the padre's visits.

One day their Bible-reading brought them to the parable of the Prodigal Son, and Andrew followed with interest the story of the young man who demanded his share of his father's wealth and then went away into a far country and wasted his money in riotous living. When his money was gone and he was utterly destitute he thought with longing of his father's home and decided to return. Feeling that he had wronged his father beyond forgiveness, he was prepared to become a servant in his father's house, but, to his joy and amazement, his father forgave him all and took him back as a son.

When they had finished reading, Andrew looked searchingly into the face of the padre. "That story could have been written for me. Did you choose it purposely?"

"Yes, Andrew, I did," replied the padre candidly. "The Lord Jesus told that story to illustrate the love of God, our heavenly Father, towards the sinner. You've wandered away from God, Andrew, and like the Prodigal Son you've sinned against Him. But He is waiting, so lovingly and anxiously, for you to repent of your wrong-doing and return to Him."

Andrew dropped his gaze and stared at the floor.

"Does God really love like the father in the parable?" he asked huskily.

" 'God so loved the world, that He gave His only begotten Son, that whosoever believeth in Him should not perish, but have everlasting life,' " quoted the padre gently.

Andrew raised his head and met the older man's kind look.

"Yes, padre, but surely God doesn't allow sin to go unpunished. If we've done wrong, we deserve to be punished. If God doesn't punish our sin it's as if—as if it didn't matter."

"Sin does matter, Andrew. It matters a great deal. God abhors sin so much that nothing sinful is allowed to come into His presence."

Andrew looked puzzled.

"But just now you said that God was waiting to receive sinners. If nothing sinful can enter His presence, how can a sinner come to Him? How can I, with all that I've done, just come to Him and expect Him to take me back as if nothing had ever happened?"

The padre turned the pages of his Bible and read slowly, "Jesus said, I am the way, the truth, and the life: no man cometh unto the Father, but by Me." He closed the Bible and leaned forward. "Do you see, Andrew, God so loved the world He allowed His own dear Son to take the punishment for our sin, that we might go free. When the Lord Jesus died on Calvary He made it possible for God to forgive us."

Andrew's face lighted up.

"That whosoever believes that the Lord Jesus died for him need not perish, but have everlasting life. That means if I believe that the Lord Jesus died for my sins I can go to God and claim forgiveness."

"That's right, Andrew; but it doesn't end there, you know. The Lord Jesus rose victorious over death. He is alive to-day and *we* can know His power to live victoriously if we surrender our lives to Him and ask Him to walk with us day by day. Won't you ask Him into your life—now, Andrew? Tell Him that you are truly sorry for all that you have done wrong in the past—believe that He died to cleanse you from your sin—and then ask Him into your heart and life, that through His power you may live a new life for Him."

Without hesitation Andrew slipped to his knees, and the padre knelt beside him. From a full heart Andrew prayed for forgiveness and asked the Lord Jesus to come into his life as Saviour and Friend and make all things new. As he prayed it seemed as if the very presence of his Saviour filled the cell and entered his heart, but when he opened his eyes and rose to his feet there was no-one to be seen but the kindly padre, who, sensing that Andrew would like to be left alone for awhile, withdrew with a promise to return the following day.

From then on life for Andrew was very different. The bitterness and burning sense of injustice that he had felt faded away and in its place came a quiet resolve to serve the rest of his sentence patiently and then start life afresh.

"What are you going to do when you leave here, Andrew?" the padre asked him one day.

"I really don't know, sir. I've thought about it many times, but I've no clear plan in my mind. I feel I must just wait and see where God leads me."

The padre, who by this time had grown very fond of Andrew, was thinking seriously of the young man's future and was determined that this "brand plucked from the burning" in such a dramatic way should be given every opportunity to live a full and useful life for God.

But there were many weary weeks and months of imprisonment to endure before Andrew would know again the sweet blessing of freedom. At times the seeming hopelessness of his position almost made him despair, and then he would turn quickly to his Saviour, to find there the comfort and strength he needed. The frequent visits of the padre, who never came empty-handed, but brought with him books and papers which he knew would interest and instruct his young friend, did much to break the drab monotony of prison routine, and the talks they had together led Andrew deeper and deeper into the Christian life.

CHAPTER FIVE

THEY TRY AGAIN

"WE don't seem to be getting very far with our detective work," observed Sheila, a few days after the picnic. She and Peter were sitting on the wide window-seat of one of the rooms overlooking the cottage. The trees, thick with foliage, made an effective screen, and little could be seen of the cottage and its inhabitant, but occasionally they heard the deep barking of the dog as some unwelcome tradesmen entered the garden gate.

Since their day on the moors the weather had broken and it had rained incessantly; but it was a soft, driving rain that held the warm promise of summer. A missel-thrush, perched on the topmost branch of a tall tree near the window, was pouring out his heart in song and telling the world that sunshine lay behind the low, grey clouds. Even as Sheila and Peter pressed their faces against the window to get a glimpse of the songster, a rift appeared in the clouds and a bright shaft of sunlight pierced the greyness.

"Oh, Peter, look!" breathed Sheila.

Every tree and bush and flower was laden with raindrops that hung, clear and sparkling, in the pure light. A passing breeze gave the branches a playful touch that set the raindrops dancing and turned each one into a scintillating rainbow before it fell, reluctantly, to the ground. The break in the clouds gradually became a large patch of brilliant blue sky and soon the garden was bathed in sunshine.

But Sheila and Peter had not waited to watch the transformation. At the first sign of sun they had run off to don stout shoes and raincoats and were already out-of-doors.

Mr. Arnold, too, had been tempted out by the brightening weather, and as Sheila and Peter strolled past his gate they noticed him busily digging in his garden. Peter called out a cheery "good-morning," and Mr. Arnold, who appeared to be in a slightly more amiable mood, returned his greeting.

Feeling encouraged, the two retraced their steps and stood looking over the gate.

"Isn't it a lovely morning?" continued Peter conversationally.

Mr. Arnold answered that it was in a tone that clearly implied he had no wish to discuss the weather further.

"What are you planting?" asked Peter, who by this time had unlatched the gate and, closely followed by Sheila, had walked up to where Mr. Arnold was digging.

"Seeds," Mr. Arnold retorted curtly. "Now go away; I'm busy."

But his two visitors appeared not to have heard, and Peter, who had learned quite a lot about gardening from Jake, continued to chat in a friendly and knowledgeable way. In spite of himself, Mr. Arnold was impressed and interested, and before long the two were deep in conversation, discussing the merits and demerits of some flowering-shrubs that Mr. Arnold had recently bought. Sheila stood by, afraid to speak, in case she should break the spell Peter seemed to have cast.

Bruce, however, had no such scruples. Hearing voices in the garden, he rushed to the window of the room where he was shut in, barking furiously, and the spell was broken. The familiar, cold expression crept back into Mr. Arnold's face, and picking up his tools he irritably told the children to run away and stop wasting his time. Thus dismissed, Peter and Sheila sauntered off, feeling that they had at least made a little progress towards getting to know their neighbour.

The holiday was going all too quickly for Sheila. Only another week remained, and feeling that she was neglecting Margaret, she asked that she might invite her friend to Southernwood again. Permission was readily given, and the following afternoon Sheila and Peter greeted Margaret when she arrived and bore her off to the far end of the lawn, where tea was laid beneath the shady elms. Nanette, Mrs. Carliss and Peter's mother were already there, seated in deck-chairs, and soon they were joined by Dr. Glennie and Sheila's father. When tea was over Nanette turned to Peter.

"We've not heard you play for a long time," she said in gentle reproof; "you will be getting out of practice."

Obediently Peter rose, and, going into the house, fetched his violin. Tucking the instrument under his chin, he lightly touched the strings with the bow, and as the lovely clear notes flowed out, Mrs. Glennie caught her breath and looked quickly at her husband. He was watching Peter, a look of quiet satisfaction on his face. Margaret, sitting cross-legged on the grass, was fascinated. It was the first time she had heard Peter play and she sat bewitched. Nanette, her small foot tapping in time to the rhythm, leaned back in her chair, smiling gently, while Sheila gazed dreamily into space and saw a world of beauty whose colour and movement and form were part of the music she heard. Another listener, unseen by the group under the elm-trees, paused in his gardening as the first strains of music reached him.

The gay melody, lilting with the youth and freshness of

spring, changed softly, almost imperceptibly, to a note of wistful yearning, until it seemed the violin spoke with a human voice. Fuller and deeper the notes probed the depths of longing, then mounted swiftly in poignant sweetness, as if seeking and searching for something beyond reach. As the last note trembled on the air and died away, the listeners under the trees breathed sighs of pleasure and appreciation; but in the heart of the solitary listener was a feeling of almost intolerable loneliness.

With angry impatience Mr. Arnold threw down his gardening tools and called to Bruce, then, slamming the garden gate behind him, he set off for a brisk walk to try to rid himself of disturbing thoughts.

Peter, with mock gravity, bowed to the applause of his audience, then, putting his violin carefully into its case, he sat down on the grass.

"It's time for someone else to entertain," he declared; "what about a story, Father? You promised to tell us about some of the African children in your hospital."

Dr. Glennie thought for a moment.

"Tell them about Kodjo," suggested Peter's mother.

"Oh, yes," exclaimed Dr. Glennie, and settled himself more comfortably in his chair while the three children gathered closer in anticipation.

"Kodjo is about the same age as Sheila," he began, "and is the only son of an important Chief whose tribe lives many miles from the mission hospital. It was, a little less than a year ago, a very backward and primitive tribe, full of witchcraft and superstition and strange, cruel customs. In fact it was the effects of witchcraft that caused Kodjo to be brought to us. He had an eye infection that was treated by the village witch-doctor in such a dreadful way that instead of getting better it became much worse, until the Chief thought that his little son was going blind. Greatly alarmed, he brought Kodjo to the white man's hospital, and after long treatment we were able to save Kodjo's sight. Every day in the hospital ward Kodjo heard the Gospel story, and after a time he became a Christain and yielded his heart to the Lord Jesus. When he eventually went back to his own people he told everyone about his Saviour and through him his father was converted and the whole life of the tribe was changed. The chief asked for a missionary to be sent to them. The people were eager to hear more of the Saviour Who loves them and died for their sins, and now, a year later, they have built a church and a school. They have turned completely from witchcraft with all its darkness and evil and are worshipping God. It is the Chief's wish that one day soon Kodjo will come to England to be taught in one of our schools, so that when he is Chief in his father's place he will make a good and wise ruler and will lead his people further into the Christian way of life."

"Well done, Kodjo," cried Peter when his father had finished; "he makes me more determined than ever to be a missionary."

Margaret listened intently while Dr. Glennie described the life and work of the mission hospital. He told them more about the little patients in the children's ward and of the loyal, willing African nurses and workers who were showing their love for their new-found Saviour by their devoted service to their fellow countrymen.

A little breeze blowing in from the sea caused Nanette to shiver and draw her wrap closely round her, and, seeing this, Dr. Glennie suggested that they should all return to the house, when he would show them a colour film he had taken of the mission work in Africa. They needed no second bidding, and made their way to the study—that being the easiest room to darken. The heavy curtains were drawn across the window and the portable screen put into position. Then for an hour they watched as Dr. Glennie showed them picture after picture of African life, keeping up a running commentary as he did so. First there were scenes of the hospital. The nurses, busy about their tasks, looked up to smile, and the patients waved from their beds. Several of the children, almost fit and ready to return to their homes, were running about the hospital grounds, and amongst them was Kodjo, the little hero of their story. He beamed as the camera focused on him, then ran off to join his companions. Next they were shown the dense, almost impenetrable jungle. Some views were from the air and showed vast stretches of jungle unbroken but for the silver blue ribbon of river that flowed through it; others were close-ups of the thick undergrowth, with grasses towering above the missionaries as they forced a way through. Then, in company with the missionaries, they visited the neighbouring villages and watched as treatment was given, medicine dispensed and, always, the Gospel preached. Southernwood was left far behind, and they were deep in the heart of Africa, taking part in its life and work. Finally they were brought back to the hospital, and Kodjo walked straight into the camera and, it seemed, into the room where they were sitting. He was so real they could see the merry twinkle in his eyes and the gleam of his dark brown skin, then, with a wave, he was gone and the film came to an end.

There was still half-an-hour to spare before Margaret had to leave, so they gathered round the piano and, with Sheila's father playing, they had a sing-song of hymns and choruses. To finish, Dr. Glennie replaced Mr. Carliss at the piano and taught them some African choruses. Old Jake, busy about his duties, listened and smiled. What a lot the old house could tell of years gone by! Romance and gaiety; quiet happiness and the sweetness of a child's voice and laughter; heartbreak and parting and the long, silent years when the old house and an ageing man shared their memories. Jake smiled again as a fresh burst of song and laughter came through the open window. The old house was happy now, truly loved and truly home.

It was such a lovely evening that Sheila and Peter decided to walk home with Margaret. The soft, sweet smells of spring came to them from the fields and banks as they walked. Everywhere was a shimmer of blue and green where bluebells flowered beneath the tender foliage. The woods that clothed the hillsides were full of bird-song and as they stopped to listen, the clear, haunting note of the first cuckoo came to them from the valley below. Looking back, they were almost dazzled by the last rays of the setting sun. Bank on bank of golden clouds were piled high in the western sky as the sun sank out of sight over the horizon. The sea, almost motionless in the still air, mirrored the loveliness of the sky and lay blue and golden in the evening calm.

Margaret was unusually quiet, but the other two, busily talking, seemed not to notice. Her thoughts were full of all she had heard and seen during the afternoon and evening. The story of Kodjo, the film, the vivid account that Dr. Glennie had given of life in the mission hospital and his description of Africa with its background of mystery and witchcraft had made a deep impression. It was a glimpse of a life she had never known existed. Up to now her own life had been one of conventional respectability. Her parents moved in a bright, modern set who found satisfaction in a round of pleasure and entertainment. Margaret had on many occasions accompanied her parents and had enjoyed the glamour and glitter of an evening's entertainment, but now, against the background of the life she had just seen, such things appeared trivial and empty. Sheila's family had something that was deep and lasting.

For a long time that night Margaret lay awake seeing again the pictures that Dr. Glennie had conjured up so vividly. The steaming jungle beneath a brilliant sky, exotic plants and strange wild life; primitive mud huts with dark-skinned inhabitants curious and eager, yet many of them still fearful and held in the grip of evil and ignorance. She saw, too, the white mission hospital, set like an oasis of healing and cleansing in the midst of suffering and sordidness, and she knew that she wanted to be there helping with all the work that needed to be done. Dr. Glennie had said they needed nurses. It would be years before she could start training properly, but in the meantime there must be something she could do. She would see Dr. Glennie again and ask him. Still planning, Margaret fell asleep and dreamed that she and Kodjo were walking through a dense forest towards a light that grew brighter and brighter. What the light was Margaret never knew, for just as they reached the edge of the forest she awoke to find the morning sun streaming through the window on to her bed.

CHAPTER SIX

THE BROKEN FRIENDSHIP

IT was the last day of the holiday.

"What shall we do to-day, Elf?" asked Peter as they sat under the old oak.

"Do you think we ought to pay Mr. Arnold another visit?" replied Sheila. "We don't seem to be getting very far."

Peter looked dubious, remembering their previous visits. "I don't think we shall do much good," he stated; "he's an awfully hard nut to crack."

"Still, I think we ought to try," Sheila persisted, and reluctantly Peter agreed.

Looking far bolder than they felt, they walked up the path to the door of the cottage and knocked politely. Their knock went unheeded, and after a pause they tried again, with as little success. The cottage appeared silent and deserted.

"He's out," said Sheila in a disappointed voice. "Let's go round to the back; we might find some clues."

"What sort of clues?" teased Peter. "Do you expect him to leave a bundle of marked bank notes lying around?"

But Sheila was not to be deterred, and set off for the back of the cottage.

"Look!" she exclaimed suddenly, and pulled Peter into the shelter of a large bush.

Mr. Arnold, half bent beneath the weight of a sack he carried on his back, was making his way to a large stone outhouse at the end of the garden. Silently they watched him enter the building and then emerge without his load.

"I'm sure it's the stolen money," whispered Sheila excitedly.

"Silly," retorted Peter. "Do you think he would put it in such an unsafe place?"

"He might have hidden it under a loose flagstone," replied Sheila, her imagination running away with her. "Anyway, I'm going to see." And keeping in the shelter of the bushes, she crept towards the outhouse, followed by a very sceptical Peter.

Mr. Arnold had disappeared into the cottage, and after waiting a few minutes to make sure he was not returning, they left the shelter of the bushes and slipped into the shed. It was dim and musty inside, and at first they could hardly make out the vague shapes standing against the walls and in the corners.

"That's strange," whispered Peter, peering round; "there's no sack here. What's he done with it?"

"Perhaps he's put it in the loft," suggested Sheila, moving towards a ladder that stood nearby. "There's a small room up there where we used to store apples."

"Right," exclaimed Peter, swinging himself on to the ladder; "let's go and investigate."

Reaching the floor above, he stooped down to give Sheila a helping hand, then, dusty and dishevelled, they stood together on the creaking boards that formed the rather insecure floor of the loft. The roof was low and sloping, and Peter could scarcely stand upright. The place looked totally neglected, and certainly very different from the days when Sheila and her mother had lived in the cottage. Thick dust lay over everything and heavy cobwebs hung from the rafters and across the small window.

"Ugh!" ejaculated Sheila as a huge black spider darted across the floor in front of her and she stepped back in alarm.

"Look!" cried Peter suddenly, "there's the sack over there!" He pointed to a dark object in the far corner.

Carefully avoiding the cobwebs, they crossed the floor-boards and, reaching the sack together, thrust their hands inside.

"Oh," exclaimed Sheila in dismay as she withdrew a hard, round object.

Peter, looking at a similar object in his own hand, snorted in disgust, then roared with laughter.

"A potato," he chuckled. "A fine pair of detectives we are!"

"It does seem hopeless," said Sheila dejectedly as she made her way down the ladder to the floor below. Brushing the dust from her blazer and skirt, she waited for Peter to descend before opening the door.

"Peter!" she gasped as the door refused to move, "the door is locked!"

"Only stuck, I expect," replied Peter calmly. "Let me have a try."

But the door resisted their combined efforts, and after several minutes of fruitless struggling they realised that they were indeed locked in.

"Do you think Mr. Arnold saw us come in and locked us in purposely?" asked Sheila fearfully.

"Shouldn't think so," returned Peter. "But let's hammer and shout and ask him to let us out."

They hammered and shouted until their knuckles were

sore and their voices hoarse, but no-one heard them. The out-house was some distance from the cottage, and the walls and doors were thick and stout. Peter looked around to see if he could find a way out, but the only window was small and set high in the wall.

"It's no good," declared Peter at length, "we will just have to wait until someone comes along."

The moments ticked by slowly until the hands of Peter's watch pointed to twelve o'clock—then half-past.

"It will soon be lunch-time," said Peter ruefully. "They will be getting anxious about us at home."

Again they hammered and banged and shouted, but they might have been marooned on a desert island, they evoked so little response.

"Oh, Peter," said Sheila, wearily sitting down on a box, "this is all my fault. I'm so sorry."

"Rubbish," retorted Peter briskly. "We're in this together. Who was to know the door would be locked like this?" And he gave the door another shake.

Just then a strange snuffling noise held their attention. It stopped, then came again from the direction of the door, followed by a long, low growl.

"It's Bruce," exclaimed Sheila. "Oh, Bruce, good dog; go and fetch your master." And she started to beat on the door again.

At the sound of Sheila's voice the dog's growl turned to furious barking, and a few minutes later the two prisoners heard footsteps hurrying down the path and a key inserted and turned in the lock.

"What is it, Bruce?" they heard Mr. Arnold say as the heavy door swung open slowly. "What is in there?"

Mr. Arnold's face when he saw Sheila and Peter standing

inside his shed was a study. Amazement, anger and something like fear appeared in quick succession.

"Get out," he snapped; "get out and don't ever come on my premises again or—or I'll set the dog on you."

In vain Peter tried to apologise, but Mr. Arnold brushed his apologies aside and repeated his order to go, while Bruce, straining under his master's grip, snapped and snarled in a menacing manner.

Sheila would have liked to take the short cut through the laurel hedge into the grounds of Southernwood, but she quailed under Mr. Arnold's furious stare and meekly followed Peter round the cottage and out of the front gate.

"Whew!" breathed Peter when they were safely outside, "what an ogre!"

"He's a horrible man," exclaimed Sheila, near to tears. "I'm more sure than ever that he stole that money, and we can't do a thing about it. It just isn't fair."

"Cheer up, Elf," consoled Peter; "something might turn up yet. Come on, I'll race you to the house. We won't be so late after all."

The run restored Sheila's good humour, and they arrived, breathless and laughing, to find the adults, also late, just returning from inspecting the new tennis-courts that were being laid at the back of the house. Thankful that no awkward questions were asked, Peter and Sheila had a hasty wash and brush-up before entering the dining-room.

"Promise me you won't go to the cottage on your own while I am away," urged Peter later that day, and Sheila readily promised. She had no wish to meet Mr. Arnold or Bruce again for a very long time.

Monday morning found Sheila cycling along the familiar

road on her way to school. In the playground Margaret was waiting for her and came hurrying to meet her as she put away her bicycle. There was little time to talk before school commenced, but during the morning break Margaret confided to Sheila her ambition to become a nurse and, one day, a medical missionary. Sheila was delighted and immediately exclaimed, "Why don't you come over and talk to Uncle John about it? I know he'll be pleased to help you."

A few days later Margaret rather shyly entered Dr. Glennie's study. Peter's father drew forward a chair for her.

"So you want to be a nurse, Margaret," he began kindly. "Why do you want to become one?"

Margaret, a trifle disconcerted by the direct question, answered, "I—I don't quite know why. When I heard you speaking about the mission hospital it seemed so wonderful and—and I felt I'd like to do something useful with my life, not just have a good time and live for myself."

Dr. Glennie nodded. "I see," he replied thoughtfully. He paused, then went on. "You know, Margaret, nursing isn't an easy or glamorous job; it calls for a lot of self-denial and hard work."

"Yes, I know," answered Margaret quickly; "I've thought of all that, but it would be so——" She hesitated, feeling for the word she wanted.

"Worthwhile?" suggested Dr. Glennie.

"Yes," replied Margaret eagerly. "I feel I could do so much good if I were a nurse and a missionary."

"There's more to becoming a missionary than being a good nurse, Margaret," said Dr. Glennie quietly.

Margaret looked surprised.

"How do you mean?" she inquired.

"I mean that you must know the love of the Lord Jesus in your own heart first, before you can go and tell other people about Him. Do you know Him, Margaret?"

Margaret looked puzzled and confused.

"I don't know," she answered slowly. "I—I don't think so. I've never really thought about it."

"Why not think about it now?" suggested Dr. Glennie gently. "It's a wonderful thing to know the Lord Jesus as your Saviour."

The puzzled expression in Margaret's eyes deepened.

"I believe in God and I go to church—sometimes. Isn't that enough?"

Dr. Glennie took a small Bible from his pocket and opening it he said, "You believe in God. Let's start from there, shall we? The Bible tells us that God is holy and perfect in all His ways; it also tells us that we are very sinful and that nothing sinful can ever come into the presence of God."

"But how are we sinful?" interrupted Margaret. "I don't do anything very dreadful. There are lots of girls at school much worse than I am."

"Anything that comes short of God's perfect standard is sin, Margaret. Selfishness, bad temper, untruthfulness, lack of love towards others and—self-righteousness. All these things are sin in God's sight just as much as those dreadful crimes we read about in the papers. In fact, the faults which we excuse and think unimportant are the seeds from which more dreadful things grow."

Margaret began to fidget. She had expected praise for her noble ambition, not a lecture. Her voice was stiff with pride and disappointment as she said, "You don't think I'm good enough to be a missionary."

"Margaret," remonstrated Dr. Glennie, "I didn't say that, my dear. You misunderstand me. I am just trying to show you that the most important thing is to get right with God, and then to think about serving Him."

But Margaret had risen from her chair and crossed quickly to the door. She objected to being preached to and, anxious to end the embarrassing interview, said in a hard little voice, "Perhaps I made a mistake. I don't think I should make a good missionary, after all."

Sadly Dr. Glennie watched her go, then dropped his head in his hands and prayed silently.

Outside, Sheila was waiting to hear the result of the interview, but when she saw Margaret's set, white face she exclaimed in dismay, "Why, Margaret, what is the matter?"

"Everything's the matter," retorted Margaret angrily. "I've just been told I'm sinful and not good enough for your precious missionary work."

"Oh, Margaret, I'm sure you've got it all wrong," answered Sheila. "Come back and have another talk." She laid her hand persuasively on her friend's arm, but Margaret pulled away from her.

"I'm going home," she said shortly; "and please don't come with me. I want to be on my own."

With a perplexed frown on her face, Sheila watched her friend hurry down the drive, then she turned and walked slowly into the house. She found Dr. Glennie still in the study, and sitting down in the chair just vacated by Margaret, she told him of what had taken place.

"I know, my dear," replied Dr. Glennie quietly. "She is like a great many other people. They cannot see that in God's sight we are sinful and that the first step in the Christian life is to get right with God. But pray for her, Sheila. She is hurt and angry now, but presently she will see things differently, I feel sure."

At school the next day Margaret carefully avoided Sheila, arriving just before lessons began and leaving immediately they finished. During the break she joined her former friends, who seemed quite pleased to have her back again, and whenever Sheila tried to speak to her she turned away. The same thing happened the next day and the following. Margaret rebuffed every effort that Sheila made to be friendly. It seemed that the break between them was final, and Sheila sadly watched her friend slip back into her old life and way.

CHAPTER SEVEN

THE ACCIDENT

S H E I L A sat on the upturned box in the greenhouse and watched Jake busy with his plants. It was Saturday afternoon, and missing the company of both Peter and Margaret, she was wondering what she could do to pass the hours until tea-time.

Since Peter had returned to school she had been left very much to her own resources. Her parents and Nanette were kept busy looking after the visitors who had started to arrive, and Dr. and Mrs. Glennie had gone North for a few weeks to attend an important convention and to visit various friends and relatives.

Idly she teased Smoky, who had slipped through the half-open door while Jake's back was turned.

"Jake," said Sheila suddenly, "I've got a secret."

Jake laughed.

"A secret's not a secret when it's told, Missy," he reminded her.

"I know, Jake, but you are different; a secret's safe with you."

The old gardener smiled at the compliment.

"All right," he said good-humouredly, "go ahead. What is it you want to tell me?"

"It's about Mr. Arnold next door. Do you know he's really the one who stole all that money that the escaped convict was blamed for taking?"

Jake turned from what he was doing and looked at her in amazement.

"What fairy-tale have you got into your head now?" he demanded.

"It's true," insisted Sheila, and told him about her encounter with the escaped prisoner on the moor.

Jake looked serious, far more impressed by Sheila's escape from danger than by the convict's story.

"I should forget it, Miss Sheila," he said kindly. "They all say they didn't do it when they are caught, and Mr. Arnold looks a respectable gentleman enough. A bit stern, perhaps, and stand-offish, but not the sort to go around stealing money. No, Missy, I should get that notion out of your head."

Sheila was disappointed. She had hoped to find an ally in Jake, but he was clearly quite unsympathetic.

"Where's your little friend Margaret?" he asked, changing the subject, and Sheila told him what had happened.

"A pity," murmured Jake, stooping to tie back a deep red carnation that had grown away from its stake. "A great pity. We must pray for her, Missy, that she will come to know the Lord Jesus."

"That's what Peter's father says," answered Sheila. "I've got an awful lot of people to pray for now. There's Margaret and Mr. Arnold and the convict"— she counted them off on her fingers. "I pray and pray, but nothing seems to happen."

Jake looked at her quizzically.

"Perhaps things are happening that you know nothing about, Missy. Like the seeds in the ground; they take a terrible long time to show through, sometimes. God doesn't always answer our prayers in the way we expect. We must have patience and trust Him."

Sheila needed plenty of patience in the days that followed. At school Margaret still refused to have anything to do with her, and at home, remembering her promise to Peter, she carefully avoided Mr. Arnold and the cottage. The Whitsun holidays seemed a long way off, and to pass away the time Sheila looked around for a new interest.

"Why don't you try sketching?" suggested her father. "You can use some of my materials if you wish."

Grateful for the suggestion, Sheila took the sketching-block and pencils to her seat under the oak-tree and settling herself comfortably looked about for a suitable subject to sketch. Woods, fields, sea and sky lay before her, and ambitiously she began to draw. After several minutes she sat back and viewed the result rather ruefully. It was quite evident she had not inherited her father's skill. However, it was fun, and tearing off the first sketch and putting it under a stone for a safe keeping, she tried again. This time she chose a solitary elm-tree that stood a short distance away. This effort was much more successful, it really looked like a tree, and feeling quite pleased with herself, she went on sketching subject after subject.

She became so engrossed in her new hobby that at first she failed to hear the commotion from the garden next door, but suddenly she was aware that Bruce was barking and whining in a most unusual way. She stopped to listen a moment, then, deciding that the dog must be hurt and in distress, she ran through the trees to the laurel hedge and peered through. In the middle of the path Bruce, still howling dismally, was standing by Mr. Arnold, who was lying white and still on the ground.

"Oh, dear," thought Sheila in alarm, "it's Mr. Arnold, not

Bruce, who is hurt; but I can't do anything alone," and, turning quickly, she ran to the house to tell her father.

Mr. Carliss immediately found Jake and together they followed Sheila along the narrow footpath that led to the laurel hedge and, pushing their way through, went quickly to the injured man. Mr. Arnold, in the meantime, had regained consciousness, but when he tried to raise himself he groaned with pain.

"I fell off the ladder," he gasped and indicated a ladder that still stood propped against the wall of the kitchen garden. The movement made him catch his breath in pain. "I seem to have hurt my side."

Mr. Carliss looked grave.

"I think a doctor should see you before we try to move you," he advised. "Sheila, run quickly and see if Dr. Crookes is at home. It won't take you many minutes."

Sheila did as she was bidden, and when she reached the doctor's house a short distance away she was thankful to see his car standing outside. Hurriedly she told him what had happened and, opening the car door, Dr. Crookes bade her get in while he fetched a few things he might need. In a matter of minutes they were on their way back to the cottage. Sheila's mother had joined Mr. Carliss and Jake and was kneeling by the side of Mr. Arnold, who looked grey and ill.

With skilful fingers Dr. Crookes examined the injured man, then sat back and said cheerfully, "No bones broken, Mr. Arnold, but you have given your side a nasty twist, and there is a lot of bruising. It will keep you in bed for a week or two, I'm afraid." He looked up at Sheila's parents. "How is he placed? Can he be nursed at home, or shall I try to get him a bed in the hospital?"

"Oh, not the hospital," said Mr. Arnold apprehensively. "I'll be all right. I can manage."

"You can't manage," retorted the doctor, almost sharply; "you need someone to look after you."

Sheila's parents exchanged glances.

"We will look after him, Dr. Crookes," said Mrs. Carliss quickly. "We have a spare room, and I know Hannah and Betty will be willing to help me."

While the doctor and Mr. Carliss, followed by a silent and watchful Bruce, carried the injured man to the waiting car, Sheila ran ahead to tell Nanette what had happened and to help prepare the spare room.

A little later, propped up in bed and with a dainty tea-tray set before him, Mr. Arnold looked around the pleasant little room and sighed somewhat fretfully. A framed text hung on the wall facing him, and two or three attractive water-colours, no doubt the work of Mr. Carliss, were placed artistically on the remaining walls. Crisp muslin curtains billowed gently at the open casement windows, through which he caught a glimpse of the distant sea. Near at hand, on a small oval table, stood a bowl of roses, and on these Mr. Arnold's gaze lingered in appreciation. Pink and cream, deep red and apricot, were reflected in the dark, polished surface of the table. Next to the bowl of flowers was a pile of books, magazines, a train and bus time-table and a small black Bible.

Hearing him stir, Bruce rose from where he was lying by the side of the bed and thrust his cold nose into his master's hand. Mr. Arnold looked down at him.

"Hullo, old faithful," he said and reached out to caress the dog's head, but even that slight movement caused him a sharp stab of pain and he leaned back wearily on his pillows.

During the days that followed, Mr. and Mrs. Carliss were kindness itself, and took every moment they could spare from their many duties to see that the invalid was comfortable and happy, but Mr. Arnold remained weary and listless, and made little progress, in spite of all their efforts.

Dr. Crookes, seeing their concern, tried to reassure Sheila's parents. "It's probably the shock of the fall. Keep him quiet, as you have been doing; and see if anything is worrying him," he added thoughtfully. "Sometimes anxiety can retard a patient's recovery."

For several days Mr. Carliss spent more time with the sick man to keep him company and to try to win his confidence, but with little response. All he could learn was that many years earlier Mr. Arnold had quarrelled with his family, of whom now only a widowed sister remained. Sometimes Sheila would stay and chat with the sick man. She was still rather scared of him, although he looked different lying pale and helpless in bed, but he spoke kindly to her whenever she entered his room, and after a few days she began to lose her nervousness. Mr. Arnold found himself looking forward to Sheila's brief visits and contrived to lengthen them by asking her questions and finding her numerous little tasks to do, until Sheila forgot her fears and was soon chatting happily about her school and her plans for the Whitsun holidays. Bruce at first retreated to the far side of the room when Sheila entered, and would lie with his head on his paws, growling softly, but a word from his master would silence him, and soon he was taking Sheila's presence for granted. In fact he and Sheila very quickly became firm friends, and when school was over Sheila would take him for long walks through the woods and lanes.

It would be hard to say who enjoyed the walks more: Bruce as he nosed and snuffed through the long grass and chased the furry creatures that fled before him, or Sheila, who once again had a companion to share with her the joys of the countryside she loved. Occasionally Sheila, who had discovered Mr. Arnold's liking for flowers, would pick a small posy and take it back to the sick man. One day, returning from a visit to Secret Cove, she and Bruce made their way slowly through the lovely wood adjoining Southernwood. The late afternoon sun slanted through the trees, casting patterns of light and shadow across the narrow footpath. From the cool, green depths of the wood echoed the voices of hundreds of birds, and Sheila sat down on a fallen tree-trunk to rest and listen. The soft, damp smells of the wood came to her as she sat. Somewhere, near at hand, was a bed of violets and, scenting their fragrance, Sheila looked around her. In a shady hollow, almost hidden from view, she espied their purple heads, and, thinking of Mr. Arnold, she left her seat and kneeling down commenced to pick a large bunch. Bruce, too full of energy to stay still for long, went off on a journey of exploration, and when Sheila had finished her task he was nowhere to be seen. But he came quickly at her call, and together they returned to Southernwood.

Begging a pale green bowl from Hannah, Sheila made her way to Mr. Arnold's room, closely followed by Bruce. Mr. Arnold's eyes lit up with pleasure when he saw the violets.

"You spoil me, my dear," he smiled, and watched Sheila as she crossed the room and, placing the bowl on the window-sill, began arranging the flowers.

Engrossed in her task, Sheila began to hum softly to herself.

Her voice was still immature, but it held a remarkable sweetness, and Mr. Arnold smiled as he listened.

"That's a very pretty tune you are singing," he observed. "What is it?"

Sheila, almost unaware that she had been singing, looked up with a smile. "It's something Uncle John taught us when he was here," she answered and, still busy with the flowers, she started to sing again.

> "In my heart a song of joy I'm singing,
>   Christ my Lord has set the joy-bells ringing.
>   For in love He took away my sin,
>   Purged its stain and gave me peace within.
>   Now each day the joy-bells ringing
>   Set this heart of mine a-singing,
>   Christ is King."

Sheila finished arranging the violets and stood back to study the effect.

"Uncle John made up the words and Peter composed the tune," she informed the sick man.

"Peter—is that boy who was with you when you—er—came to visit me?" he asked.

Sheila blushed at the memory of their unwelcome visits.

"I think I owe you both an apology," continued Mr. Arnold. "I was very rude to you. Will you forgive me, my dear?"

"Yes, of course," Sheila responded warmly. "We were very rude, too. It was wrong of us to trespass on your property as we did."

Mr. Arnold chuckled.

"You were a persistent pair," he commented.

Later that evening Sheila sat writing her weekly letter to Peter.

"I think I must have made a mistake about Mr. Arnold," she wrote. "He seems really nice, and Bruce is a dear. We are great friends."

CHAPTER EIGHT

MR. ARNOLD WRITES A LETTER

AFTER Sheila left him Mr. Arnold lay gazing out of the window, the catchy tune and words of the chorus she had sung ringing in his head:

> "For in love He took away my sin,
> Purged its stain and gave me peace within."

Mr. Arnold had never prayed in his life before, but something like a prayer rose to his lips. "If only that could be true of me." he murmured wistfully.

He had been brought up in a home where little thought or time had been given to spiritual things. Life for his parents had been one long struggle against poverty, and young Alec Arnold, revolting against the squalor and drabness of his lot, decided early to make his way in the world. He had worked and studied at a night school to remedy the defects in his education and, thus equipped, he had left his home and found work in the large town nearby. From there he moved to London and obtained a responsible post with a large firm; promotion followed, and with it security and freedom from the nagging fear of poverty. But somehow he failed to find satisfaction and happiness. In his struggle for success he had had no time to make friends and he had wandered so far from his family that they were practically strangers. He had returned home twice, once when his father died and again shortly afterwards when his mother, worn out with months of nursing a sick husband, collapsed and slipped quietly away to join him. His widowed sister with her two unruly children had gone to live in the shabby little house he had once called home, and there she eked out her pension by working for people in the village. Depressed by the poverty of it all, Alec Arnold had speedily returned to London. From there he sent a small regular sum of money to his sister, but he never again returned. Looking back over the long years, Mr. Arnold sighed at their emptiness and frustration.

The daylight was fading, and outside the lovely landscape lost its bright colours and became shadowy and dim, but Mr. Arnold made no effort to switch on the little lamp that stood conveniently near. A gentle tap on the door disturbed his reverie, and Mrs. Carliss entered, bearing a tray on which was a hot drink and some biscuits.

"Shall I switch on the light?" she asked him cheerfully, but Mr. Arnold demurred, saying that he preferred the twilight. Thinking that he was half asleep, Mrs. Carliss withdrew with a quiet "Good night."

But Mr. Arnold was not asleep. He lay awake staring into the swiftly falling darkness. The trees stood in black outline against the sky, and one by one the stars appeared. The moon rose slowly and turned the familiar garden into a world of silver and black. In the nearby woods an owl hooted, accentuating the lonely stillness of the night, and the moon rose higher, flooding the little room with light. It touched the violets that Sheila had placed on the window-sill, the bowl of roses and books on the table; it fell on the water-colours that hung on the wall and lit up the text facing Mr. Arnold. "Peace I leave with you, My peace I give unto you," he read as he drifted off to sleep.

When Mr. Arnold awoke, the birds were beginning their glorious dawn chorus. From every tree in the surrounding woods they twittered and chirruped, then burst into such a hymn of praise that the whole sky seemed full of song. The sick man stirred, and opening his eyes saw again the text that had been his last waking thought. He sighed contentedly, but even as memory returned a shadow crossed his face. Such peace could never be wholly his.

The daylight strengthened and the rising sun touched the waters of the bay with golden splendour. The cool, sweet freshness of the early morning drifted in through the open window and brought to him the lovely fragrance of Sheila's violets. He turned to look at them, and as he did so his glance fell on the little Bible by his bedside. Stretching out his hand, he picked it up and began to turn its pages. So engrossed did he become in what he read that not until Hannah entered with his breakfast tray did he put the little book down again.

That morning when Mr. Carliss paid his usual visit to the sick man he found him with the Bible in his hand.

"I see you are reading the best of all books," he said genially as he pulled forward a chair and sat down.

"Yes," replied Mr. Arnold, his voice husky with emotion. "I only wish I had started reading it sooner. Indeed, if I had had this book placed in my hands when I was a youngster my life would have been very different." He sighed regretfully. "But it's too late now."

"Why do you say that?" asked Mr. Carliss gently.

"I've not given God one thought all these years; it's not likely He'll have much interest in me now."

"You are wrong, you know," replied his companion. "God is always ready to receive those who come to Him."

"Not when they've spurned Him all their lives."

"Even when they've done that," rejoined Sheila's father. Mr. Arnold looked interested.

"You really mean there is hope for me? That I can have a part in—in all this?" He indicated the Bible in his hand.

"Yes, indeed," replied Mr. Carliss. "If you are willing to take the Lord Jesus Christ as your Saviour; if you believe that He died for your sins."

"Sins!" Mr. Arnold shivered. "My sins are too great for God to forgive."

"There is no sin so great that it cannot be cleansed by the blood of the Lord Jesus."

"Are you sure?" asked Mr. Arnold eagerly.

"I'm positive, man," replied Mr. Carliss emphatically. "The word of God says it, and I've proved it."

Mr. Arnold leaned back on his pillows.

"You really mean that sin can be wiped out and we can start again?"

"That's what the Bible says." Mr. Carliss took the Bible from Mr. Arnold's hand and quickly turned its pages. " 'The blood of Jesus Christ His Son cleanseth us from *all* sin.' "

He turned the pages again. " 'Repent ye therefore, and be converted, that your sins may be blotted out.' " He looked at Mr. Arnold. "The Bible is full of such assurances of God's forgiveness if we are penitent." Taking a pen from his pocket, he underlined several more passages, then handed the Bible back to Mr. Arnold.

When Sheila's father left him, Mr. Arnold picked up the little book and carefully read the portions that had been underlined.

The following day when Mr. Carliss visited him Mr.

Arnold was very quiet and pre-occupied, and thinking that perhaps the sick man was too tired to talk, he rose to leave, but he had scarcely reached the door when Mr. Arnold called him back. "I want to write a letter," he said. "Could I trouble you for some writing materials?"

"Certainly," was the courteous reply, and after fetching writing-paper, envelopes and a pen, Sheila's father helped Mr. Arnold to sit up, then left him to his writing. With difficulty, for his side was still giving him considerable pain, Mr. Arnold drew the writing-paper and pen towards him, and after a moment's thought began to write. Carefully re-reading what he had written, he folded the sheet of paper and placed it in an envelope. This he sealed and addressed to Mr. Carliss. When Sheila's father returned later in the day Mr. Arnold handed him the letter.

"Will you take this and put it in a safe place?" he asked. "If anything happens to me—if I die—open it and act on the instructions inside. If I get better I want it back again."

Sheila's father took the letter and, promising to carry out Mr. Arnold's request, put it in his pocket until such time as he could lock it in the safe.

"You are not going to die," he assured the invalid; "the doctor says you will be well again in a week or two if you make the effort."

"I don't know if I want to get well," was the listless response.

But, in spite of himself, Mr. Arnold did get well. Each day after writing the letter saw an improvement in his health, and soon the loving care that was showered upon him began to have effect.

CHAPTER NINE

MARGARET SEES THINGS DIFFERENTLY

AFTER parting with Sheila, Margaret soon found herself caught up in a whirl of gaiety again. Her friends included her in all their social activities and her parents encouraged her in her search for pleasure and a good time. At first she enjoyed it immensely. It was fun being popular, and the gay life which her parents and their friends lived held great attraction for her; but after a while the round of pleasures began to pall and Margaret found herself beginning to long for the quietly happy days she had known with Sheila. Sheila was so different from everyone else. She did not go to endless shows and theatres, but she was always happy. She seemed to have found a source of happiness that never let her down. At one time Margaret had wondered what had changed Sheila so completely during the past year, but since her visits to Southernwood she was beginning to understand.

Seated in front of her dressing-table, getting ready to accompany her parents to the theatre, Margaret recalled some of the times she had spent at Southernwood, and in particular her talk with Dr. Glennie. A feeling of shame swept over her as she remembered her rudeness. Dr. Glennie had been right: she did not love the Lord Jesus. She believed in Him in a vague sort of way, but she did not love Him as Sheila and Peter did.

Meanwhile, Sheila was being kept very busy at home and

had little time to think of anything but her many duties. With an invalid to look after as well as caring for the other guests, Mrs. Carliss had her hands fully occupied, and Sheila helped in every way she could. When she could do no more for her mother she would take Bruce for a long walk and then stay and chat to Mr. Arnold, who was proving a most entertaining companion.

Margaret, in spite of her desire to renew her friendship with Sheila, was too shy and embarrassed to make the first move, and Sheila, little knowing how Margaret was feeling, made no further effort to win back her friend. Each day Margaret determined to speak to Sheila, but each day her courage failed her, and a week passed without the friendly overture being made. Then quite simply they were brought together again; it was the occasion of Margaret's thirteenth birthday.

Several weeks before, when Margaret had been enthusiastic about missionary work in Africa, Sheila had bought a book of African adventure as a birthday present and now, on the morning of Margaret's birthday, Sheila was in a quandary. Should she still give the present to Margaret? She would probably be rebuffed, and Sheila disliked the thought of being humiliated in front of the other girls. Still undecided, she put the book, wrapped in gaily coloured paper, in her school satchel. Perhaps there would be an opportunity to give it to Margaret when no-one else was about.

It was not until school was over for the day that such an opportunity occurred. Sheila was wheeling her bicycle out of the school shed when Margaret went by, unaccompanied. Quickly Sheila called out to her, and Margaret retraced her steps.

"Happy birthday, Margaret," ventured Sheila nervously. "I've been wanting to give you this all day, but I haven't had the chance;" and she held out the present.

Margaret took the parcel without a word and stood looking at it for a long moment; then, when she raised her eyes, to Sheila's surprise, they were full of tears.

"Margaret, you're crying!"

"Oh, Sheila, I've been hoping and hoping we could be friends again, and I've been too proud and silly to ask you. Will you forgive me for being so horrid?"

Sheila's look of pleasure was the only answer Margaret needed, and arm in arm, chatting as if there had never been a break in their friendship, the two walked down the drive-way to the school gates.

When she reached her home Margaret went quickly to her room and untied the precious gift. Written on the fly-leaf, in Sheila's round, clear handwriting, were the words "To a future missionary"; and as Margaret scanned the pages of the book all her longings and ambitions came flooding back. She sat on the edge of her bed and day-dreamed. The familiar bedroom faded away, and in its place she saw the long, airy wards of the mission hospital with its dark-skinned patients and happy, smiling workers. She saw Kodjo with his beaming face and mischievous eyes. With Dr. Glennie and his wife she went through the steaming jungle to the distant villages, and there she watched the missionaries give medical treat-ment and heard them tell the beautiful Gospel story. She heard again Dr. Glennie's voice as he spoke to her during that fateful interview when she had lost her temper and quarrelled with Sheila. He had said that bad temper and pride were two of the sins that separated people from God, and

Margaret could not deny that she possessed both of these. But Kodjo had found the way to God; he had taken the Lord Jesus as his Saviour.

Margaret looked down at the book in her lap and idly turned its pages. There were coloured photos of African scenery, reminding her of the film Dr. Glennie had shown them, pictures of gaily-clad native women with round-eyed piccaninies on their backs, and, further on, illustrations of witch-doctors surrounded by a weird and frightening medley of evil-looking charms and idols. Margaret's eyes sparkled with excitement. She *would* be a missionary when she grew older. The thought of adventure and the difficulties to be overcome thrilled her, but this time she would set about it the right way. She would learn from Sheila and her family more about the Lord Jesus and His love. Closing the book, Margaret knelt down by her bedside and prayed her first real prayer: that God would teach her and guide her, in His way.

Almost before they realised it the Whitsun holidays were upon them and Sheila and her family were looking forward with eager anticipation to the return of Dr. and Mrs. Glennie and Peter. Mr. Arnold, who was now practically recovered, suggested, not very enthusiastically, that he should leave. Mr. and Mrs. Carliss would not hear of it, and told him he must stay until he was really well. Nothing loath, Mr. Arnold accepted. The cottage was going to seem very lonely and quiet after the bright company of Southernwood.

At first Peter eyed Mr. Arnold and Bruce rather warily, not quite sure of his reception, but after a while he confessed to Sheila, in some amazement, that they seemed completely changed.

"What have you done to them?" he questioned.

Sheila laughed.

"It must be Southernwood's soothing influence."

Bruce immediately transferred his affections from Sheila to Peter, much to Peter's delight and Sheila's chagrin.

"You old turn-coat," she accused him indignantly.

Margaret was once more a frequent visitor to Southernwood, and she lost no time in seeking another talk with Dr. Glennie. This time she left the study with a radiant face.

"You look as if you have found a fortune," exclaimed Peter as Margaret joined them on the sunny terrace.

"I have," answered Margaret happily. "I see things quite differently now, and I'm going to live for the Lord Jesus from now on."

"Bravo, Margaret," said Peter quietly, then he jumped to his feet. "This calls for a celebration. Let's go and ask for a picnic."

"Oh, Peter," exclaimed Sheila, half laughing, half reproachful; "you're never at a loss for an excuse for a picnic!"

"I love 'em," stated Peter as if that were the only excuse needed and, still laughing and talking, they made their way into the house.

In a secluded spot a few feet away Mr. Arnold put down the newspaper he had been reading and, lying back in his deck-chair, closed his eyes. The warmth of the sun fell on him gently, and all around were the soft, incessant sounds of early summer. Above in the vivid, blue sky a snow-white gull cried plaintively; but Mr. Arnold heard only the echo of Margaret's words—"Live for the Lord Jesus."

CHAPTER TEN

DOING THE RIGHT THING

I N the kitchen an indulgent Hannah and Betty stopped in the middle of their many duties and packed Peter's haversack with all the good things needed for a picnic. Bruce, who had no intention of being left out of the celebrations, followed the children around hopefully, so a bottle of water and a small dish were included for him. Then, their preparations completed and their parents informed of where they were going, the little group took the path that led to the moors above Southernwood.

A few hours later, the good things in the haversack practically demolished, the trio relaxed. Bruce, his tongue lolling, had flopped in the shade of a large boulder and lay, head on paws, watching their every movement.

"What a pity we couldn't bring Smoky with us," commented Margaret; "it seems a shame to leave him out of things."

The other two laughed.

"I don't think Smoky would appreciate the climb," observed Peter.

"Do you remember how we first met Smoky, Peter?" asked Sheila; "it's nearly a year since we rescued him."

"I most certainly do," replied Peter with feeling. "I got a sprained arm for my pains and missed the music exam."

"What happened?" asked Margaret, looking interested.

Between them Sheila and Peter recounted how they had

saved Smoky from being drowned by a band of rough boys from the village.

"It was just after that that you decided to be a missionary," Sheila reminded Peter.

Peter, his chin resting on his knees, nodded thoughtfully.

"Yes, that makes two of us. What about you, Elf? Are you going to be a missionary, too?"

"I don't know. I don't know what I want to be." Sheila looked at her two friends rather enviously. "I wish I could be as decided as you two."

"Will you become a doctor like your father, Peter?" asked Margaret.

"Yes," responded Peter, without hesitation, "and you are going to be a nurse." He turned to Sheila and said persuasively, "Won't you support the medical profession, Elf?"

But Sheila shook her head.

"No, I don't want to be a nurse," she answered.

Bruce left the cool shadow of the rock and came to where they were sitting. Flopping down by Margaret's side, he rested his head in her lap and looked up with such a comical expression that they all laughed merrily.

"Do you want a romp, Bruce?" asked Margaret, stroking his head. "Do you think we have sat still long enough?"

As she moved, the sunlight caught the silver bracelet on her arm, and not for the first time Peter glanced at it curiously.

"It's a charm bracelet," explained Margaret, following his glance; "it's supposed to bring me good luck." She held out her wrist for a closer inspection.

Peter nodded slowly.

"Yes, I know. But now you are a Christian do you think you ought to wear it?"

Margaret looked at him in surprise. He was looking straight back at her, and for a moment she was struck by his likeness to his father.

"Why not?" she queried.

"Well," Peter went on, "don't you think that trusting in charms shows a lack of faith in the Lord Jesus—as if we think He can't take care of us completely?"

"I see," said Margaret slowly. "I hadn't thought of it that way." She slipped the bracelet from her wrist and looked at it lying in her hand. "I do trust the Lord Jesus," she said simply, "utterly and completely and to prove it—there!" She threw the glittering trifle as far away into the heather as she could.

Peter looked at her in admiration, and Sheila clapped her hands in approval. Not to be outdone, Bruce rose to his feet and barked excitedly, scattering a pair of jackdaws that were hopping around looking for crumbs.

"All right, Bruce, old boy," exclaimed Peter, "we're going home now. Here's a stick to carry." He held out a short, thick piece of wood, which the dog immediately took in its strong jaws. "That will keep you quiet."

Laughing, the three jumped to their feet and, picking up the litter they had scattered around, they began the long descent to Southernwood. Bruce, still firmly grasping his prize, walked ahead with solemn dignity.

The following day Mr. Arnold announced that it was time he returned to the cottage. He was quite fit again and it was unfair to trespass further on the kindness and hospitality of his host. Seeing that he had really made up his mind, Mrs. Carliss offered to see that the cottage was ready for occupation and to order a supply of groceries from the village.

Mr. Arnold voiced his appreciation.

"You put me further and further into your debt," he told her. "I shall never be able to repay all your many kindnesses."

"We are going to miss you, sir, when you go," said Peter sincerely. He and Sheila were sitting on the lawn near Mr. Arnold's chair, idly rolling a ball to and fro in front of Bruce's nose.

"But we can come and visit you, can't we?" asked Sheila eagerly. She looked up with a roguish smile. "You won't set Bruce on us, will you? It wouldn't be much good now!"

Mr. Arnold joined in the laughter that followed.

"No, my dear, that I never will. I'm ashamed to think that I ever threatened such a dreadful thing."

"We were rather a nuisance," admitted Peter; "it was unpardonable of us to trespass as we did."

"But things are different now. We are all friends, aren't we, Bruce?" said Sheila, putting her arms round Bruce, who looked up at her adoringly.

Mr. Arnold, looking at them, felt a sudden pang of regret, and wished with all his heart that he was worthy of this trust and friendship.

"What's the matter, sir?" asked Peter quickly, noticing the expression of pain that crossed Mr. Arnold's face.

"Nothing, my boy, nothing very much," replied the other with difficulty, but after a few minutes he rose from his chair and walked slowly into the house.

"I'm sure he's ill," said Peter, looking after him. "He looked so queer. Do you think I ought to fetch Father?"

Reaching his room, Mr. Arnold locked the door behind him and, crossing to the window, dropped heavily into a chair. Then began the greatest battle of his life.

After several minutes he hid his face in his hands and

murmured brokenly, "Dear God, give me the strength to do the right thing."

A hurried knocking on the door caused him to sit up, and Dr. Glennie's voice called to him, "Are you all right, Mr. Arnold? May I come in?"

Rising, Mr. Arnold crossed the room and unlocked the door.

"Yes, perfectly all right—now, Dr. Glennie." He spoke calmly, and Peter's father looked at him keenly, but the gaze that met his was serene and untroubled.

It was Nanette's suggestion that they should all meet together in her drawing-room that evening for a kind of farewell party for Mr. Arnold, but to Mr. Arnold himself it seemed almost like the guidance of God.

The evening drew to a close, and the banter and chatter had died down to a companionable silence when Mr. Arnold turned to Sheila's father and said quietly :

"Will you let me have that letter I gave you some time ago, Mr. Carliss?"

"Of course," replied Mr. Carliss promptly. "I'd forgotten all about it. I'll go and get it now," and jumping to his feet he left the room, returning a few minutes later with the letter in his hand.

"There you are, sir," he exclaimed, and would have handed it to Mr. Arnold, but the older man stopped him.

"I want you to open it and read it."

Surprised and somewhat mystified, Mr. Carliss did so, then looked at Mr. Arnold as if he could not believe what he had read.

"It's true, man," said Mr. Arnold, his voice firm and resolute. "Read it out for the others to hear."

Mr. Carliss sank into his chair and passed his hand across his forehead before reading aloud:

" 'I, Alec Arnold, wish to make known——' " and then followed a most amazing confession. Mr. Arnold was guilty of the crime for which Andrew Tennant was serving a prison sentence. Details of false evidence were given and then the statement that the stolen money, still untouched, was locked in the safe in "Southernwood Cottage."

"Now you know what sort of person I am," said Mr. Arnold when Mr. Carliss had finished reading. "Utterly unworthy of all your kindness," and his voice shook.

He looked round at the circle of faces staring at him, but it was on Sheila and Peter that his look lingered. He expected to see them shrink away in dislike and horror, but their eyes were shining.

Sheila crossed quickly to his side.

"Oh, I'm so pleased you've owned up," she cried. "I knew God would answer our prayers."

Peter followed closely and seizing Mr. Arnold's hand exclaimed, "I think it's jolly decent of you, sir."

Almost overwhelmed, Mr. Arnold got out shakily, "Thank you, my dears. That is going to mean a great deal to me in the days ahead." He turned to the adults, who were still almost too stunned to speak. "You of course realise fully what this means. I shall have to get in touch with the police and notify them of the facts, and then take whatever punishment is coming to me."

"Does that mean you will go to prison?" asked Sheila in an awed voice.

"Yes, my dear; but don't worry about me. I shall have

some wonderful memories to take with me, and"—he looked wistfully at the others—"I hope some good friends to come back to."

"Indeed, yes," exclaimed Dr. Glennie, the first to recover from the shock which Mr. Arnold's confession had given them, and he gripped Mr. Arnold's hand firmly. "It's not an easy thing that you have chosen to do, but we are your friends and we will stand by you."

It was a sad and subdued group that gathered together in Nanette's drawing-room to say farewell to Mr. Arnold the next morning. Mr. Arnold was the most composed of all. Now that he had committed himself to putting right the great wrong he had done there was a peace and joy in his heart that even the thought of the approaching interview with the police and the punishment that would surely follow could not dim.

He looked round at their anxious faces.

"Don't grieve for me, my friends. Whatever the future holds I shall have One with me to comfort and sustain me, and I can also look forward to the joy of meeting you all again."

Bruce, as if sensing the long separation that lay ahead, kept close to his master's side.

"I'll take care of him while—while you're away," promised Sheila.

"And I'll write to you, sir," offered Peter.

"Jake and I will keep your garden in order," put in Mr. Carliss, while Nanette and Sheila's mother promised to keep the cottage spick and span ready for its owner's return.

With a catch in his throat Mr. Arnold thanked them all,

and then Dr. Glennie asked for silence while he commended Mr. Arnold into God's safe keeping. With a final pat for the faithful Bruce, Mr. Arnold, accompanied by Dr. Glennie, climbed into the car that was waiting for him and was driven away.

CHAPTER ELEVEN

SHEILA MAKES A DISCOVERY

IT was surprising how quickly life at Southernwood returned
to its normal routine. Peter went back to school and Dr.
and Mrs. Glennie went to stay at an hotel in London to be
within easy reach of Peter's school and also more central for
their work.

Bruce at first missed his master sadly and moped around
the house looking forlorn and heart-broken, but everyone
petted and spoilt him, and even Smoky showed himself willing to be friendly and agreeable.

A few weeks after Mr. Arnold's departure Sheila was on
the lawn playing with Bruce and Smoky when a bright red
sports car swept up the drive and drew to a standstill before
the open front door. A very immaculate young man jumped
out of the car and ran up the short flight of steps. Sheila
watched curiously as he turned to speak to someone in the hall.
It was her father, and to Sheila's surprise he called to her. She
scrambled to her feet and made her way to where her father
and the stranger were standing.

"Someone to see you, Sheila," said Mr. Carliss.

Sheila looked at the young man blankly, failing to recognise
him.

"You don't remember me," the stranger smiled, but at the
sound of his voice recognition came to Sheila—and she stared
at him incredulously.

"I look a bit different from what I did when we met before," laughed the young man, and Sheila, finding her voice at last, agreed.

Mr. Carliss was looking from one to the other as if seeking an explanation.

"It's a long story, sir," said the visitor, "but I would like to tell you, if I may," and Mr. Carliss led the way into the study.

In the privacy of the study Sheila and her father listened intently to Andrew's story.

Beginning with his weak and foolish behaviour that ran him heavily into debt, he explained the circumstances that led up to the theft of the firm's money and how easy it had been for Mr. Arnold to throw the blame on to his, Andrew's, shoulders, and how although he had protested his innocence he had been unable to prove it.

"I broke out of prison thinking I could persuade Mr. Arnold to confess. It was a futile and stupid thing to do, but at least one good thing came of it." He paused, then continued, "I met Sheila. She made me think very deeply, and I realised that although I was innocent of the crime for which I was being punished, I was guilty of quite a lot of other things."

Sheila interrupted him eagerly.

"Do you remember your promise?"

"Indeed I do. In fact I started to keep my promise long before I had any hope that God would answer your prayers for me." He looked from Sheila to Mr. Carliss. "I've given my heart and life to the Lord Jesus and, with His help, I am going to live for Him. In fact I have already made inquiries about studying for the ministry."

Mr. Carliss, who all this time had been a silent and very interested listener, leaned back in his chair, and when he spoke his voice was very serious.

"You know, Sheila, you should have told your mother and me about all this. It was very wrong of you to keep quiet."

Sheila hung her head at the rebuke.

"Yes, I know, Daddy," she murmured, almost inaudibly. Reproof from her father was more than she could bear.

Andrew came quickly to the rescue.

"It was really my fault, sir. I asked her not to say a word to anyone."

"Very well, we will say no more about it," replied Mr. Carliss and, reaching over, he lifted Sheila's downcast face with his hand.

"I'm really rather proud of my little girl," he said, smiling. "It must have taken quite a lot of courage to act as you did in such a terrifying experience."

"I quite agree," put in Andrew heartily. "I must have looked a frightful sight with several days' growth of beard and my clothes all muddy and torn."

Sheila laughed, her high spirits restored by her father's praise.

"You did look rather dreadful," she admitted.

For the next few weeks Andrew, who was staying with Margaret and her parents, was a frequent and popular visitor to Southernwood, and when one day he informed them that his holiday was nearly over and that he must soon return to London, they felt a keen sense of loss.

"I did so want Peter to meet you," said Sheila in disappointment.

"I'll be back during the summer holidays," promised Andrew. "But I must return to London now. I've been accepted by the training college, and there's a lot I have to do before I can start studying in the autumn."

The weeks sped by and the long, summer holidays grew steadily nearer until at last the day came when Peter and his parents returned to Southernwood.

Dr. and Mrs. Glennie's stay in England was drawing to a close. This would be the last holiday they would have at Southernwood for several years, and everything was being done to make it as happy and enjoyable as possible. Peter spent most of his time with his parents, and spoke often of the day when he could join his father on the mission-field.

"You are looking a long way ahead, Peter," said his father kindly. "You have years of study in front of you yet."

"I know," replied Peter, "but it's great to have something so worthwhile to study for and look forward to."

Sheila listened to the conversation rather wistfully. What was she going to do when school days were over? Try as she might, she just could not make up her mind. Leaving Peter and his father still talking, she wandered off by herself, and her steps led her to the old oak that had been her retreat for so many years. Pensively she sat looking out over the familiar scene. The rolling countryside was rich with the gold of harvest. On gently sloping hills the corn stood straight and still in the hot summer air, and in the valley the orchards gleamed with their burden of fruit. Whatever the season Southernwood looked beautiful, and Sheila knew in her heart that she never wanted to leave it. For her the excitement and adventure of foreign lands held no appeal. Whatever her work for God might be, she hoped it would be here, in the quiet loveliness of the English countryside.

She was so deep in thought she did not hear Peter approaching, and not until he dropped lightly by her side was she aware of his presence.

"You look sad, Elf," he said gently.

"No, Peter, not really sad," she smiled, "only thoughtful. Just wondering what I am going to do with my life. The rest of you seem so very decided, but I just can't make up my mind to anything."

"I shouldn't worry, Elf. When God has some work for you to do He will show you."

The conversation drifted to other subjects. Peter spoke of his life at school and described various meetings he had been able to attend with his parents, while Sheila in turn told him about Andrew.

"He promised to come again during the summer holidays. I hope he remembers."

Andrew did remember. In the stifling heat of London he thought often of the fresh beauty of Southernwood and the wide expanse of moors that stretched high above the sea. There was much to do before he could make his promised return visit, but he looked forward eagerly to the day when he could leave the crowded city behind. He had visited Mr. Arnold, and although their talk together had been very brief and far from private, he had assured him that he felt no bitterness about the past. All was over and forgiven, and when Mr. Arnold returned to the cottage Andrew promised to visit him there.

As usual, the holidays went all too quickly. Sheila, Margaret and Peter, with Bruce in close attendance, roamed far and wide through the lanes and woods. Bathing parties and picnics, in which many of the visitors joined, were organised, and in the evenings Peter would play his violin. Usually it was the lovely music of the old masters, but occasionally he would play a piece of his own composition. Sheila loved these little pieces of Peter's; they seemed to capture the haunting beauty and serenity that pervaded Southernwood.

One evening, just as Peter finished delighting his audience with his playing, a red sports car flashed past the window.

"It's Andrew, I know it is," cried Sheila, and ran to the door to meet him. On the doorstep stood a smiling Andrew accompanied by an equally happy-looking Margaret. After Andrew had been introduced to Peter and his parents, and while the adults were busily talking, Sheila, Margaret and Peter slipped out to look at the car.

"Isn't she lovely?" asked Margaret.

"She's a beauty," agreed Peter and walked slowly round the car, examining it with the air of an expert.

"Well, young fellow," said Andrew's voice behind him, "would you like to go for a ride in her?"

Peter swung round. "I sure would," he breathed—"do you mean now?"

Andrew nodded.

"Oh, super!" exclaimed Peter. "I'll just go and ask the parents if it's all right," and he was half way into the house before Andrew's voice reached him.

"There's no need. I've already asked for the lot of you. Hop in."

With Peter sitting in front beside Andrew and Sheila and Margaret in the back they drove off. Along lanes where the trees almost met overhead, past fields of scarlet poppies and golden grain, down into the valley where the orchards were heavy with fruit and the cottage gardens ablaze with michaelmas daisies and dahlias, then up and up to the moors that stretched purple and gold in the evening sunshine.

After driving for about an hour Andrew turned left

towards the sea and home. The road took them along the cliff-top, and far below they could see the surf breaking on the beach. Jutting out to sea, the black rocks made a perfect background for the gleaming white gulls that wheeled and dipped with breathtaking grace and ease.

"Let's stop here, just for a few minutes," begged Sheila, and, eager to prolong the pleasure of the outing, the others agreed. Andrew swung the car on to the grass verge and as he pulled to a stop they all clambered out. Going as near the edge of the cliff as they dared, they sat down on the short, springy grass and revelled in the loveliness of the summer evening.

"Tell us about your plans, Andrew," invited Peter, when there was a lull in the conversation. "Are you all ready for college?"

"Yes, all ready, Peter. I start at the beginning of the new term in just over a week. Almost the same time that you all go back to school."

"Are you going to be a missionary?" asked Margaret with interest.

"No, I don't think so," replied Andrew. "I want to be a prison padre."

"You are all so sure of what you want to be," sighed Sheila. "I wish I knew."

Andrew looked at her. "But you've already found your mission, Sheila. You are working while the rest of us are still talking about training."

"How?" queried Sheila, pleased at Andrew's words, but not quite understanding their meaning.

"By witnessing for the Lord Jesus wherever you go. It is through your prayers that I came to know Him, and it is so with Mr. Arnold."

"Me, too," said Margaret quietly. "It was because Sheila lived for the Lord Jesus at school that I first began to realise that there was more to life than having a good time."

"There you are, Sheila," exclaimed Peter. "You are a missionary already."

Sheila felt a little glow of happiness inside her. So this was her work for God : just to quietly witness for Him wherever she went.

The westering sun sank behind a bank of billowing clouds and touched each pinnacle with golden glory. The little group on the cliff-top shaded their eyes from the dazzling light that streamed from the heart of the sunset.

"How wonderful!" breathed Peter in an awed voice.

"It's like a glimpse of the Golden City," said Sheila softly.